Rachel

COLLEGE TERRACE BRANCH

Palo Alto City Library

6/89

Also by Ruth Wallace-Brodeur

THE KENTON YEAR
(A Margaret K. McElderry Book)

One April Vacation

One

RUTH WALLACE-BRODEUR

A Margaret K. McElderry Book

April Vacation

ATHENEUM   1981   NEW YORK

LIBRARY OF CONGRESS CATALOGING IN PUBLICATION DATA

Wallace-Brodeur, Ruth
    One April vacation.

    "A Margaret K. McElderry book."
    Summary: Nine-year-old Kate, sure she will die in one week
because she has pulled out a nose hair, decides to make her last
week a good one.
    I. Title.
PZ7.W15883on   [Fic]   81-3568
ISBN 0-689-50211-7

Copyright © 1981 by Ruth Wallace-Brodeur
All rights reserved
Published simultaneously in Canada by McClelland &
Stewart, Ltd.
Composed by American–Stratford Graphic Services, Inc.
Brattleboro, Vermont
Manufactured by Fairfield Graphics,
Fairfield, Pennsylvania
Designed by Maria Epes
First Edition

To Sarah Blythe

One April Vacation

Harlan Atwater once told Kate that if for any reason a hair came out of her nose she would die within one week. This didn't sound right to Kate, but Harlan swore it was true, it was just not many people knew about it because it rarely happened. Nose hairs, he said, were attached very securely. Kate had never even noticed she had hair inside her nose and thought only a few bushy sorts of men did.

Anyway, she didn't think about it again until one Sunday afternoon in April, at 2:47 o'clock. She was sitting on her porch steps picking her nose and just happened to notice a tiny hair sticking out of the piece on the end of her finger. She sat there staring at it and she felt a little sick, because she was remembering what Harlan had said.

"How stupid," Kate thought as she rubbed her

finger against the edge of the step. "Harlan was just teasing me."

But that was exactly what was worrying her. Harlan never teased. He was in her sister Alison's class in junior high and he didn't joke around. He was very smart and very serious. Kate kept thinking about how smart Harlan was and how he read all the time and never played kickball after supper with the neighbor kids. He probably knew lots of things nobody else knew because of all that reading. Once she had seen him get *Science Journal* out of the library. Maybe he read about nose hairs in there.

Kate sat on the steps a long time. She had always been nervous about the thought of dying, but it was hard to imagine it really happening to her, especially when she was perfectly healthy and always had been, especially for such an odd reason as a missing nose hair. If she had to die, she would rather it be from something like a tropical blood disease that she had caught nursing a stricken jungle tribe. She would lie, wan but beautiful, in a darkened room with ceiling fan, while weeping family and friends hovered nearby attending her every need. Grateful natives would fill the yard, begging the gods to spare their saviour even as she gasped her last breath. The gods, miraculously, would hear . . .

"She is dying of a lost nose hair." Oh no! Who, even in their darkest grief, would not feel just the slightest desire to laugh? Hadn't she giggled inside when their milkman told them his sister-in-law had been run down by a truckload of coffins?

There was nothing she could do about it. In the long run, what did it matter? The end result would be the same. If she died, there would be no more Katherine Cullen Sardis of 148 Willow Street, daughter of Elizabeth, sports equipment designer, and James, history teacher at Newberry Junior College. Kate wondered how long it would be before her parents went back to work and Alison returned to her mobs of admirers at the junior high. Would they miss her sadly forever? Or would Alison in time come to enjoy the benefits of being an only child? She said often enough she wished she was one.

Just then Kate saw Harlan Atwater walk by on the sidewalk across the street.

"Harlan!" she yelled. "Hey Harlan, wait a minute." She jumped up and sprinted after him. Harlan half turned, but kept walking.

"Do you remember what you told me about dying if you lose a nose hair?" Kate asked breathlessly.

"What?" said Harlan, still legging it up the street.

"You said a person would die if a nose hair came out. Was it true or were you lying?"

"Do I look like a liar?" asked Harlan, and he turned up his walk and disappeared into his house.

What did that mean? Was it true or not? Of course not. Kate *knew* it was not true. And yet . . .

Kate walked slowly back toward her big yellow house. It would do no good to talk with her parents, because she knew for sure they'd never heard of such a thing. Nothing they did or said could be any help.

In a week she would know one way or the other. That was a long time to wait for an answer of this sort.

K ATE DIDN'T HAVE much chance to think about her problem that evening because the family went to watch the annual soap-box derby on Scanner Hill, but the next morning it was waiting like a gray mist when she woke.

"You're awfully quiet," her mother said at breakfast. "Anything the matter?"

"You can tell just by looking at her there's a lot the matter," said Alison as she helped herself to Kate's uneaten bagel.

"People are going to need a wide-angle lens to look at you," retorted Kate, watching the last of her breakfast disappear into her sister's mouth, and the subject of her silence was lost in an exchange of good-natured insults.

When the breakfast dishes were done, Kate went out and sat in her usual spot on the porch steps. It was spring vacation and the weather knew it. Forsythia hedges glowed up and down the street and the sun had warmed the stone steps under her. Larry Rooney, the horror from next door, walked by chewing on a wad of gum as large as a rubber ball. Kate wondered where he got it. He used to pick it up off the sidewalks. She supposed he didn't do that anymore—after all, he was older than she was—but you never could tell with Larry.

Larry was the bully of Kate's early years. Among other things, he had dropped her swing chains down the sewer, slashed her bicycle tires with his new Boy Scout knife, and tossed her birthday sailboat through his cellar window.

Larry's mother was a huge barge of a woman who forged up the street once a day in her bedroom slippers to the corner grocery. She glowered at anyone who let slip a pleasant greeting and was not the least concerned about her son's atrocious behavior. When Kate had summoned her courage to knock at the Rooneys' front door and report the loss of her sailboat, Mrs. Rooney had bellowed a string of unrepeatable remarks, ending with "and get the hell out of here." Kate had, astonished that Larry's mother spoke the same language as he did. Her parents had already learned the futility of such appeals.

There was no Mr. Rooney around. Kate figured

he probably took one look at Larry and left for good. But lots of grown brothers and sisters, old enough to be on their own, hung about the house getting into fights that could be heard for blocks. Old Mrs. Dreyfus, who lived on the other side of the Rooneys, called the police on such occasions. It didn't do any good. Mrs. Rooney yelled at them too.

Kate sighed. Even the thought of never seeing the Rooneys again was no comfort to her now. Larry didn't bother her much anymore anyway. In fact, he seemed to like her, which in a way was worse, considering the sort of kid he was. The turning point had come when Kate punched him in the nose. Larry had directed his nastiness at Mrs. Dreyfus that day, releasing the latch on her clothespole so that her laundry collapsed to the muddy ground. Mrs. Dreyfus had been enraged to the point of tears, and Kate had been sent to help repair the damage. On the way over she passed Larry, looking very pleased with himself. When he took aim at her through the V of his sling shot, she quite deliberately shot her fist into his nose.

It was the first time Kate had ever hit anyone like that and she was amazed at the results. She was amazed at the blood spurting down over Larry's mouth and chin and she was amazed he didn't

knock her brains out but instead ran for home, bel-
lowing for that awful mother of his.

Mrs. Rooney had surged forth to scream at Kate's
back door about a monster attacking her baby. Kate's
mother, to Kate's great surprise and satisfaction, shut
the door in Mrs. Rooney's face. Great-Aunt Melindy,
who was there at the time, said, "That's the way to
do it," and took Kate to Foster's ice cream parlor
for a banana split.

That was it, Kate thought suddenly. She would
go see Aunt Melindy. Aunt Melindy always had
good ideas, and she couldn't just sit around waiting
for a whole week.

"On my seventy-fifth birthday, I decided I would eat more ice cream," Aunt Melindy said when she noticed Kate watching her lick round and round her butter almond ice cream cone. They were sitting on the bench outside Foster's. Kate regretted gobbling her own cone with so little notice when she saw the way her aunt savored each drip of hers.

"Have another?" Aunt Melindy offered perceptively.

"No, thank you." Kate refused firmly. Her problems could not be solved by ice cream.

"Of course, ice cream cannot solve problems," said Aunt Melindy as though she were reading Kate's mind, "but like a good book or a warm bath, it can make them take their place in line. Problems tend to be a bit arrogant, don't you think?"

Kate was not sure what she thought about her

aunt's comments, but as usual, they made her feel better. "Do you have nose hairs?" she asked suddenly.

"I suppose so, doesn't everyone?" her aunt answered.

"Did you ever lose one?"

"Now that I don't know. I usually don't take note of such things. Why?"

"Oh nothing. Just wondering." Kate was silent for a few moments, then asked, "Do you think about death?"

"No more than I have to. The idea does cross your mind now and then when you're as old as I am." Aunt Melindy tsked-tsked and scrubbed a dribble from her dress front.

"If you thought you were going to die, what would you do?" Kate stared down at her sneakers and waited.

"Well for one thing, I don't *think* I'm going to die, I know I am. We all are. But if I thought it was going to be soon, say in a week," Kate shot her a quick glance, "or a month or whatever, I think I'd try to finish up doing all the things I've wanted to do and haven't had time for yet. And if there weren't any of those left, because after all that's what I've been doing ever since your Uncle George died and I realized I wouldn't last forever, I would be sure to do just the things that pleased me most. I have a feeling they'd be pretty much the things I do anyway. But I might stop vacuuming—or dental flossing. I've never enjoyed either of those."

Kate nodded. That sounded a good plan to her. She had felt she should take some action, in case Harlan Atwater knew what he was talking about, but she hadn't been able to settle on what. It didn't seem right to spend her last week just sitting on her porch steps. She would spend some time doing that because she enjoyed it, but there were lots of other things she wanted to do, and she only had a week.

Kate deposited their sticky napkins in the trash can. She said good-bye to Aunt Melindy and walked slowly toward home through the spring sunshine. The three blocks between Aunt Melindy's apartment building and her own street were her favorite part of town. Besides Foster's there was the post office with its big stone steps and its endlessly fascinating pictures of criminals. Kate always wondered if she would recognize those faces in a crowd.

Next to the post office was the hardware store, then the cleaners and Mason's Pharmacy, where Kate had taken a pack of Juicy Fruit gum when she was five years old. The friend who accompanied and encouraged her had chewed all the gum and then told on her. Kate could still feel the shame of returning to the store with her mother to confess and pay up. She'd never taken another thing, even though kids at school did it all the time. For her, crime did not pay.

After the pharmacy came Manelli's Fruit Store and then Larson's Bakery. Mrs. Larson always gave Kate a big, chewy oatmeal cookie when she went in to get something for her parents. Even though she'd already had an ice cream cone, Kate decided to visit Mrs. Larson. Aunt Melindy had said to do the things that pleased you.

As she approached the bakery, Kate saw a group of boys clustered near the door. They were big boys, older than Kate, the kind she had learned to watch out for. She had concluded long ago that boys were a bit like dogs: nothing to worry about one at a time, but mean in packs.

Kate decided to postpone her visit to the bakery. She kept her eyes straight ahead and marched steadily along the sidewalk. Just as she got opposite the bakery, the group of boys split apart with bursts of high, foolish laughter. One of them was swinging something around and around above his head. Kate was clear past before she realized what he was holding.

She stopped abruptly and turned back. Yes, it

was a cat. That horrible boy was swinging a cat by its tail and all his stupid friends were laughing.

Kate walked back to the group. "Put that cat down!" she commanded.

No one noticed her. "Put that cat down!" she ordered, this time with a good deal more force.

Some of the boys turned to stare at her. "Who's gonna make me?" sneered the boy with the cat.

"Put it down!" Kate's voice startled even herself.

The boy hesitated, then tossed the cat at Kate. "Take it, baby," he said and swaggered off down the street with his friends, cackling like a demented rooster.

Kate figured the cat must belong to somebody, so she put it down on the sidewalk. "Go home, cat," she said, but the cat didn't move. Kate picked it up and went into the bakery. Mrs. Larson came from the back when she heard the bell.

"Hello, dumpling," she greeted Kate cheerfully. "How about a cookie?"

If anyone was a dumpling, it was Mrs. Larson. Great rolls of fat circled her body like rings on a stacking toy. Her breath came in wheezes, as though it had to squeeze its way through the extra flesh. Her smile faded when she saw what Kate was holding.

"That cat's been hanging around here all week, making a pest of itself. Won't let me pat it, but it sure goes for the milk."

"Then it's not yours?" Kate asked.

"No, and I don't want it to be, either. Never did take to cats." Mrs. Larson grunted as she reached into the case. "Here are two cookies if you'll get rid of it for me."

Kate couldn't believe it. A cat for her, just like that. She'd always wanted a pet, but never had one because her mother absolutely forbade it. She said they had fleas and she was allergic to fleas. If one hopped on her, she went crazy trying to catch it.

The cat seemed a little tense. Its claws were dug into Kate's jacket and its ears were pressed flat back, but it didn't try to get down. Kate made a quick decision.

"If you have a box I can put him in, I'll see what I can do," she said.

"Wonderful!" bellowed Mrs. Larson joyously. "And don't tell your Ma where you found it."

Kate refused to think about her mother and the fleas as she carried the box home. After all, this case was different. She couldn't abandon an animal like this, and she should be allowed her heart's desire under the circumstances. Aunt Melindy had said as much. And having a cat, Kate now realized, was one of her heart's most treasured desires.

She put the box down when she reached the corner of her street and peeked inside the folded flaps. The cat didn't look as good as she had remembered. His eyes were runny, and his tail was kind of skinny. In fact, he looked skinny all over, now that his fur was wet and sticky from throw-up. Apparently the milk Mrs. Larson had given him hadn't traveled well. But he was a gray striped tiger cat with a white bib, and that was Kate's favorite kind. She hoped it was her mother's favorite, too.

I T WASN'T. Kate could tell the minute her mother looked inside the box and moaned. "Oh no!"

"This cat's had a hard life," Kate said quickly. She told her mother about the boys. "And now it's sick. It wouldn't be right to turn it away, would it?"

Mrs. Sardis looked at Kate's eager, pleading face. She looked back at the miserable little cat who had made no attempt to jump from the box. She sighed. "Oh Kate, I don't know." Then, "Put the box on the porch. I'll have to think about it."

Kate could not suppress a happy smile as she picked up the box. "Thinking about it does not mean yes," her mother warned. But it did not mean no either, and Kate knew that her mother didn't keep her dangling with bad news. Not usually.

She got a clean box from the attic and lined it

with an old bath mat. She put the cat in and watched as he curled up in the sun and went to sleep. "Arthur," she decided. "If I get to keep him, I'll call him Arthur." The name had a certain dignity, and she had thought about Arthur Schumer, a boy in her class at school, the minute she noticed that the cat had been sick. Arthur Schumer threw up a lot. In fact, he had thrown up all over Kate's desk two days before vacation. Arthur was a nice enough kid when he wasn't throwing up. His mother said he had an excited stomach. Nothing really wrong, just an excited stomach. Like this cat. Kate was sure that was all that was the matter with her cat.

Arthur slept most of the afternoon. Mrs. Sardis looked out through the screen door several times at Kate guarding the wretched animal. About four o'clock she joined them on the steps. "I thought he might like some yogurt," she said. "That's easy to digest." She set a little dish next to Arthur in his box.

Arthur sat up and stretched. He tested the yogurt and decided he liked it. "That's enough for now," Kate's mother said when he had polished the dish clean. "Maybe you can try a little tuna later." She took the dish and went back into the house.

"Oh Arthur," Kate whispered excitedly. "I think you can stay." Her smile faded. And who would take care of him if the Atwater prediction came true? She wouldn't think about it. Arthur needed help now.

In the middle of dinner, Mrs. Sardis said, "If he's going to stay here, he has to have a bath."

"Mother!" Kate shrieked. "Oh I knew you would let me have him," she burbled as she dashed around the table to hug her mother.

"Oh brother," said Alison. "If we're going to have an animal, why does it have to be such a disgusting one?"

"Arthur's not disgusting," yelled Kate. "You wouldn't look too good if you'd been treated like he was. You don't look too hot anyway. I'm sorry," she said immediately. "You look fine." If something happened to her, Arthur would need Alison's good opinion.

"You sure are weird," Alison muttered, but she did stay in the kitchen for Arthur's bathtime. "Poor thing," she crooned when their father approached the sink with the trembling animal. "Cats hate water."

"He'll keep himself clean after this," Jim Sardis said as he lowered the cat into the basin of suds. The touch of water certainly perked Arthur up. He shot straight into the air and landed halfway across the kitchen. In the end, after a lengthy hunt and chase, Kate's father had to wear a raincoat and gloves to do the job, Arthur was so fierce. Kate's mother toweled him dry with an old beach towel and Alison got him a dish of tuna, while Kate fixed a bed in the corner by the cellar door.

"You and I may only have a week," she whispered to a clean but resentful Arthur, "but my family will take care of you."

$\mathscr{D}\ \mathscr{D}\ \mathscr{D}\ \mathscr{D}$

Kᴀᴛᴇ's ꜰɪʀꜱᴛ ᴛʜᴏᴜɢʜᴛꜱ the next morning were of Arthur. She found him sitting on the windowsill of her mother's workroom, staring intently through the screen at robins who hopped about in the apple tree.

"He's pleasant company," her mother said as she turned from her drawing board to give Kate a good morning hug. "And how are you today?"

"Fine," said Kate after a moment of checking. "Fine," she repeated in surprise. She had expected to feel some symptoms by now. "My nose isn't even sore."

"Did you bump it?" her mother asked.

"Only a tap," said Kate hastily. "Nothing at all, really."

"Well good," her mother said, "because you look fine. Absolutely beautiful, in fact." She smoothed

Kate's tangled brown hair away from her eyes and smiled. "You're getting your summer freckles already."

Kate peered cross-eyed down her nose, which was always freckled, but much more noticeably in summer. "I've decided to like them this year," she said. "Alison says some of her friends wish they had them and even draw them on with eyebrow pencil."

Kate fixed herself some French toast, then spent the morning following Arthur about. His stomach showed no further signs of delicacy. He had already learned where the food was kept and returned frequently to sit hopefully by the refrigerator door. He accepted everything Kate offered. Some of her French toast, a little leftover green bean casserole, a few cornflakes, and more yogurt held him until Alison brought home some tinned cat food for his lunch. Appearing reasonably satisfied for the time being, he retired to his bed for a nap.

With Arthur asleep, Kate had time to think about what she wanted to do for the rest of what might be her last week. What she had always wanted to do and hadn't had time for, Aunt Melindy had said. Things that pleased her the most.

That was not as easy as it sounded. She had always wanted to see the world, but that was impossible because of time and money. A ten-speed bike, even if her parents agreed, seemed a poor investment right now. The day had clouded over and started to drizzle, which eliminated a lot of choices for the afternoon. Kate finally decided that what she most wanted right then was for her two best friends, Mike Leno and Angie Beaudry, to come over to see Arthur and play in the attic.

Mike and Angie arrived a few minutes after Kate telephoned, because they lived just down the street. Kate figured that was partly why they were her best friends. Some of the kids at school were maybe nicer, but they didn't live close enough to play.

Mike and Angie were properly impressed with Arthur, who slept through their inspection, and Kate's story of how she got him.

"You mean you just walked up to those boys and told them to leave the cat alone?" Angie asked. "Weren't you scared?"

"I didn't have time to think about it," said Kate. Looking back, she was a little surprised herself at her courage.

Mike's respect was a bit more grudging. "I probably could have handled them," he said with off-hand bravado. "Boys like that aren't as tough as they seem."

"Oh yeah?" said Angie scornfully. "Then how come you beat it when Larry Rooney threatened to pop your soccer ball if you didn't let him play with it?"

"That was different," mumbled Mike.

"Yes," agreed Kate. "There was only one of him but *seven* boys were bothering Arthur." Even though she had acted instinctively, she had no intention of letting Mike Leno belittle her deed. It was very agreeable to be considered a hero.

Mike had regained his good humor by the time they shared some fig newtons and went up to the attic. It was dark up there. The rain had increased and was rattling so loudly on the roof they could hear nothing from downstairs. They hauled some old sofa cushions over to one of the two windows and for a while they played games and worked on a jigsaw puzzle they found jammed under a bed spring. Except for such things as Christmas wrappings and decorations, fiberboard boxes of out-of-season clothing, luggage and camping gear, the attic was a museum of the past. Baby furniture, boxes of old letters and school records, useless heirlooms, out-of-style hats and clothing all waited silently in the shadows of the attic.

As the afternoon wore on and the gloom deepened, Kate and her friends began to tire of games and puzzles. They lay staring down at the street far below, and after a while Kate started telling, in a hushed voice, a ghost story Alison had brought home from one of her pajama parties. It was a good one, full of mysterious disappearances and restless spirits seeking revenge.

"Do you believe that stuff?" Angie whispered, glancing over her shoulder into the darkening attic.

"These forces exist, whether we believe in them or not," murmured Mike with quiet authority. "I read that violence is noticed and absorbed by whatever surrounds it. The furniture, the walls, remember. The spirits involved haunt the place forever."

"You're nuts," said Kate, but her whisper didn't sound too convincing. She was remembering Alison telling her about how plants that were in the room when a murder was committed reacted in a way that machines could measure whenever the murderer came near them again.

"I'll bet this old attic has secrets," said Mike. He reached for the flashlight Kate had brought and sent the beam sweeping over dark shapes. "Probably nothing out here in the middle. We'd have to go back under the eaves."

"Want to?" Angie's giggle sounded both nervous and excited.

"Why not?" said Kate. She didn't really believe any of this, but it might be fun.

"We probably won't find actual things. Let's just

try to keep open to feelings," said Mike as he started off on all fours for the back of the eaves.

"Ouch!" yelped Angie almost immediately. Her hair had caught on a nail sticking out from one of the slanting beams.

"Hold the light, Mike," said Kate as she started to free Angie's hair. Then, "What's this?"

In her hand she held a torn shred of ribbon that had been snagged on the same nail as Angie's hair. "Put it in your pocket," Mike instructed. "We'll look at it later."

The three crawled on until Mike pulled up short. "Here's something," he said as he fixed the light on the insulation that puffed out at the ends of the floor boards. He reached his hand to where a faint gleam had caught his eye and came up with a shoe. "Let's go back to the window and take a look," he suggested.

They crawled back to their cushions around the window and held the shoe to the light. It was a high heel, a very fancy one of dirty pink satin.

"This belong to anyone in your family?" Mike asked Kate.

"No," she answered, "I never saw it before." She reached into her pocket for the ribbon. "Look at this!" she said. "It's pink satin too. Or it used to be."

"Oh no!" breathed Angie. "Do you think. . . ?"

"Of course not," scoffed Kate with more assurance

than she felt. Angie tended to go off the mark a bit easily and needed to be calmed down.

"Don't be so sure," said Mike suddenly. He had taken the flashlight and was over by the chimney, which went up the center of the attic. "What are these brown spots on the floor, Kate? Did you people spill anything over here?"

"I guess we must have," said Kate, trying to sound casual. This was getting to be too much. Angie would go into hysterics any minute now if they didn't stop. But she knew they hadn't spilled anything. What could you spill in an attic? And she knew as well as anyone that blood turned brown when it dried.

"Come on," she said. "Let's go downstairs." But Mike, who was back with them at the window, continued to send the light stabbing about the attic.

"Stop!" said Kate, grabbing his hand. "Look at that!"

The three stared silently at the frayed end of rope dangling from the highest rafter.

"I know!" breathed Angie. "It all fits! Somebody dragged her up here and hung her. Then they stuffed her body back under the eaves!"

"Could have been smugglers," whispered Mike. "Maybe she saw . . ."

"Her bones could be lying there in the insulation

right now," Kate put in suddenly in a rigidly calm voice. "I think we'd better leave."

"I can't see the stairs, and I don't want to go by the . . ." Angie began in a high whimper, when a rustling from where they had found the shoe ended all further discussion. The three friends bolted as though thrown by lightning, across the attic and down the stairs. The door at the bottom always stuck, but they burst right through it, slamming it back against the wall of the upstairs hall. They didn't pause until they got down to the kitchen, where the lights were on and Kate's parents were getting supper.

"Who's after you?" Jim Sardis asked as they piled up in a breathless stop. Kate, Angie and Mike just stood there panting. Who was after them? None of them knew what to say.

Just then Arthur came padding down the stairs and into the kitchen to sit expectantly by the refrigerator door. A cobweb dangled from his ear, and bits of grayish insulation clung to his whiskers.

Kate's racing heart began to slow. "That noise must have been Arthur," she said, choking back a wild giggle.

"What's that?" Mrs. Sardis asked. Mike was still holding the pink shoe. "We found it in the attic," Kate said. "Way back under the eaves."

"It must have belonged to the family that lived here before us," her mother said. "They had four girls."

Kate and her friends looked at each other. Maybe. But that didn't explain the blood or the rope. And what about the matching ribbon? But they didn't say any more. Parents could think up good explanations for anything. And the three friends were remembering that they had spooked themselves before in the attic telling ghost stories.

"Is HARLAN ATWATER really smart?" Kate asked Alison that evening. The sisters were both curled on the couch, reading. Their mother was bent over the card table, which she had set up near the fireplace, fiddling with an assortment of little springs, screws and wheels that she had pulled from the inside of the kitchen clock in hopes of fixing it.

"Of course he is," Alison answered. She looked up from her book. "He knows everything. He's like a human computer. He even knows more than some of the teachers."

Kate sighed. That's what she'd figured. "It's just not fair," she murmured.

"Brains aren't everything," said her mother. "It's nice to have enough to get by, but other things are more important."

"Like knowing how to fix this tent?" suggested

Jim Sardis, as he struggled through the door half-buried beneath a mound of blue canvas.

"Not me!" said his wife. "Don't look at me! I'm doing the clock. Whatever made you get that out now?"

"Got to be ready," Mr. Sardis replied cheerfully as he dumped his load by the rocker. "We'll be going to Spruce Lake early this year, and if I have to order a new zipper it might take a while to come." He sat down and began to paw through the folds of stiff canvas in search of the net door with its broken zipper. "Good thing I remembered this," he congratulated himself, "or we could have spent fourteen nights swatting bugs."

Kate felt a lump come to her throat at the sight and smell of the blue tent. Doing what she wanted this week could never begin to make up for missing things like Spruce Lake. Her family went there every summer for two weeks. It was always the same, and it was always terrific. They camped at the end of the lake in a field that was owned by friends of theirs. These friends had a cottage nearby, but as it was not a regular camping place, and as most of the lake was still undeveloped, there was hardly anybody else around.

The blue tent was huge. Alison and Kate slept in one part, their parents in another, and there was still room for other stuff. In case of rain, they put the tent up as soon as they got there. It was a long ride to Spruce Lake and everybody was always tired and silly. Everybody except Kate's dad. He was always tired and cross.

They would spread the tent out in the same level place each year, then hammer stakes into the ground to fasten down the corners and edges. Sometimes the stakes would go right in and pull right out again, and sometimes you could hammer and hammer until they were all bent up and still not in. That was the first thing that irritated Jim Sardis. He always said that field was the only one in the whole northeast made of both sand dunes and rock ledge.

When the edges were fastened down, they started on the frame. Lots of pieces had to fit together, then hook into loops on the tent. If one piece came out the whole thing collapsed and Kate's dad would say they weren't trying. They were, but by then they would also be giggling, so he never believed them.

When the outside frame was all set, Mr. Sardis would find the doorway and crawl inside to raise the center pole. It was funny to watch him move around in all that canvas, looking for the middle. Once Kate's mother said he looked like a mole searching for grubs, and he crawled back out and said if she thought it was so funny she could get in there and do it herself. Their dad had a fine sense of humor, but not when he was putting up the tent.

Sometimes he got the pole up without any trouble and then they would be almost finished, but sometimes when he pushed the pole up it made the frame collapse, even though they were all holding on like mad, and then he would yell that they weren't doing it right and they would have to start all over again.

As soon as the tent was up and Kate's bed made, she would head around the shore to their friends' cottage. There was a girl a little younger than Kate named Jill. Jill was very good at catching frogs and salamanders. The two girls spent a lot of time doing that. Alison used to come too, but last summer she had spent the entire two weeks lying on a blanket in the sun. She only got up to eat, go to bed, and grease herself with more baby oil mixed with iodine, which she said was the best thing for tanning. Kate thought she was probably more stained than tanned.

Once Kate and Jill found a frog with a broken leg. They could tell it was broken because of the way it stretched out behind, and the frog couldn't hop or swim. They had bandaged the leg to a popsicle stick and made a big cage from a box and some old window screen. Then they spent most of their time catching flies and bugs for him to eat.

They had named the frog Harvey and thought about keeping him for a pet and maybe entering him in a frog-jumping contest. But they decided he would rather live in the lake, so when Harvey's leg seemed fixed, they took him out to the point where they'd found him and let him go. At first he just sat in their hands, then when they gave him a little shove he fell into the water and just floated there. They thought maybe his leg wasn't fixed after all, but when they poked him some more he bent it and began to swim. He swam out a way, and they were feeling happy that his leg was fixed and sad that he was going when he swam back and jumped into Kate's hand.

"I guess he doesn't want to leave us," she had said, and they brought him back to Jill's cottage and put him in his box. That turned out to be a mistake, because that summer some people at the other end of the lake had a pet crow named Chester. Chester was a real pest. He stole everything that wasn't tied to the ground. His favorite game was to sit on clotheslines and pull off the clothespins. You'd find all your clothes lying in the dirt with no pins in sight and you'd know Chester had been there.

Harvey's cage was kept at Jill's cottage, and every morning, first thing, Jill would take Harvey for a walk so he could get some sun. She was so sure Harvey wouldn't try to get away that she'd walk along the shore holding him out on the palm of her hand. Chester must have had pretty good eyes, because one morning he swooped down, grabbed Harvey from Jill's hand, and flew away. Good-bye Harvey.

After that, whenever they saw Chester, they yelled and threw sticks. He didn't pay any attention, but it made them feel better.

Kate sighed. Whether you were a frog or a person, life was tricky. She just hoped it was as tricky for Harlan Atwater as it was for her and Harvey. Maybe his computer brain sometimes went on the blink.

KATE WAS too busy the next couple of days to think much about her problem, other than to notice rather cautiously from time to time that she felt fine. No weakening, no loss of appetite, no aches or twinges that she could tell.

The sun was back on Wednesday morning and Aunt Melindy called early to see if anyone would like to go fishing. Kate's mother was working at her drawing board, her father, who was on vacation that week too, was still involved in tent repairs, and Alison had arranged to shop with friends. That left Kate, who liked nothing better than to spend time alone with Aunt Melindy.

"Since it's just the two of us, let's take our bikes," Aunt Melindy suggested. "I'll pack a lunch and you get the worms."

Well before noon, the two were on their way out

of town. Kate rode her mother's old English bike and Aunt Melindy pedaled along serenely on her big three-wheeler. When the sidewalks ran out they stayed in the breakdown lane of the highway until they came to the road that branched off toward the river. The river itself was polluted by industrial waste from town, but a way up, a stream ran into it that was clean and known to have trout. Not many had been caught in recent years, but memories of past success kept a few old-timers coming back.

Aunt Melindy and Kate didn't much care if they caught something or not. In fact, they would have been more surprised than pleased if they had hooked anything worth keeping, as neither of them liked fish. "Can't think it's good to swallow all those nasty bones," said Aunt Melindy, and Kate agreed completely. No matter how hard you looked, there were always some you missed.

"Wouldn't mind taking one back to your folks," said Aunt Melindy now as they settled with books and poles on the bank. "With the price of food today, it would be good value. You and I could eat peanut butter."

Kate grinned. She could picture Aunt Melindy and herself nibbling peanut butter and crackers while Alison and her parents feasted on trout cooked with lemon and butter. If it weren't for those awful bones, the idea of fresh fish appealed even to her.

"I'm hungry," she said. "Breakfast was a bit scarce."

"Oatmeal?" asked Aunt Melindy knowingly.

Kate nodded. Her father had cooked breakfast that morning, and he firmly believed nothing started the day better than a big bowl of steaming oatmeal. It was cold, globby oatmeal by the time Kate could bring herself to eat it. She figured she'd wasted a good deal of her life staring into that scummy paste. It was the only food her father insisted on her eating. "Sticks to your ribs," he always said with satisfaction. Kate had no doubt that it would stick to anything.

"Well dig into the lunch," said Aunt Melindy. "That's what it's there for." She stood to reach back up the bank for the lunch bag, and as she did so her foot slipped on a loose stone and down she tumbled, right into the water of the swift-moving stream.

"Oh!" she gasped as she struggled to regain her footing. "Oh my!" she said as the current swept her around a rotting stump at the stream's edge. "Give me a hand, Kate dear," she called as she continued on down the stream amidst her ballooning blue cotton skirt.

After a few seconds of stunned immobility, Kate was scrabbling along the bank, frantically trying to think just how she could do that. Her aunt was moving faster downstream than Kate could run. "Swim!" she yelled. "Grab something!" She staggered over a root and almost went in herself. Her aunt disappeared around a bend in a swirl of blue. "Help!" screamed Kate to whoever might hear. "Help!"

Fighting her way through the bushes and brambles that crowded the water's edge, Kate rounded the bend and saw her aunt immediately. She was sitting peacefully in the middle of the stream and waved gaily when she saw Kate. "There you are," she called. "That was some ride."

Kate stood trembling, trying to catch her breath. It was obvious what had happened. The stream broadened and became suddenly shallow here, allowing her aunt to come to rest on a sandbar. Her relief made her weak and she sat down.

"Oh don't do that," called Aunt Melindy. "I'm going to need some help getting across to the bank. It's deeper over there."

Kate nodded. So it was. She couldn't be sure exactly how deep it was, but she thought she could walk across it. Anyway, she could swim, and the water wasn't going too fast here. She pulled off her shoes and jeans and waded in. The cold made her gasp, but she kept on across. The water reached no farther than the middle of her chest. It wouldn't come that high on Aunt Melindy. She was a tall woman.

"Come on," she said when she reached her aunt, "you'll freeze out here in another minute." She grasped her aunt's hand firmly in her own and started back across. At one point Aunt Melindy slipped but Kate held on and kept going. She'd never really noticed how light and delicate Aunt Melindy was. She'd always seemed sturdy enough to Kate, but now her hand felt very fragile indeed.

When they reached the bank Kate grabbed hold of a tree branch with one hand and hauled her aunt up with the other. "Just like a beached fish," said Aunt Melindy when she was clear of the water. Her teeth were chattering and her lips looked blue.

"Keep moving," Kate urged as she pulled on her jeans. "You've got to get dry." They struggled back through the rough to where their things were waiting in the sun as though nothing had happened. "You'll have to take off your clothes and wrap up in the blanket," said Kate as she shook the leaves and twigs from the blanket they had been sitting on.

"Don't you think. . . ?" began Aunt Melindy.

"No," said Kate firmly. "You must get those wet things off right now. It wouldn't be good to try to ride home in them in this breeze. You sit in the sun in that blanket and I'll ride home and get Mom or Dad to come back in the car."

"Do bring some clothes," Aunt Melindy called as Kate started off. "I don't intend to appear in town like this."

Kate pedaled as hard as she could and arrived home so out of breath she could hardly gasp out her story. Her parents didn't seem reassured by her opinion that, apart from the cold, Aunt Melindy was basically unhurt. As Kate changed, they dashed about collecting clothes from Kate's mother's closet and exclaiming worriedly. Jim Sardis would have been stopped for speeding had a policeman been anywhere about, but fortunately they arrived at the fishing spot without any problems.

"What ho!" shouted Aunt Melindy in greeting. "Hand over your goods, you villains." Kate giggled, but her mother asked anxiously, "Are you all right? Can you dress yourself?"

"Of course," Aunt Melindy replied. "Just took an early swim, is all. Now hold that blanket for me . . ."

Kate's mother held the blanket up while Aunt Melindy climbed into the dry clothes. "Oh I do like your taste, Elizabeth," she said when she was ready. "Makes me feel years younger. I ought to get something like this for myself."

Kate's mother grinned. "Then you're really all right?"

"Absolutely nothing wrong with me, other than hunger," replied Aunt Melindy crisply. "Being eighty-two does not mean that you collapse at every little crisis."

"I'll ride your bike home," said Kate, "then maybe we can eat that lunch you packed."

Aunt melindy and Kate chose to eat their chicken sandwiches and chocolate cupcakes out in the tent, which Kate's father had struggled all morning to erect on the back lawn, so he could be certain nothing else needed repair. Instead of using the frame, he had tied the tent loops to whatever was handy in the yard.

"I do love tents," Aunt Melindy said as she leaned back in the lawn chair Kate had brought in. "Haven't been in one for years. Not very comfortable when your Uncle George and I camped out on our trip across country back in 1947. We didn't have air mattresses or foam pads. Pretty near ruined your Uncle George's back. Then when I traveled in Spain I had an air mattress, but it always had one more leak than I could account for. Miserable business, waking every morning, if you'd managed to sleep, knowing it had let you down again. Still . . . there's nothing like sleeping in a tent." Aunt Melindy yawned and put the remains of her sandwich down for Arthur. The warmth of the tent, heated by the sun and shielded from the breeze, was making them both drowsy.

"I'll be right back," said Kate. She ran into the house and up to the attic where the camping gear was stored, returning shortly with foam pads and pillows. "Let's take a nap," she said as she spread the mattresses on the tent floor.

"Excellent idea," said Aunt Melindy approvingly, and both were asleep within five minutes.

They woke a long while later to see one corner of the tent slowly collapse in toward the middle. Aunt Melindy put a warning hand over Kate's to signal silence, then pointed to the wall toward the lowering sun. Kate could see a shadow move slowly across the canvas, then after the merest vibration a second corner folded in.

"Larry Rooney," mouthed Kate to her aunt, and imitated the action of sawing through a rope. Her aunt nodded agreement and pointed to a strip of shadow on the tent wall that was between Larry and the next rope. Kate stared, bewildered for a moment, then remembered. The broom her father had used to sweep the tent out was leaning against the wall on the outside. Quickly Kate stood up and silently wrapped her hand through the loosened canvas around the end of the broom handle. She waited as Larry's shadow crept slowly closer. He was obviously moving with the greatest care. He must have been watching them from his upstairs window and knew they were sleeping in the tent. At exactly the right moment, Kate levered the broom up. Larry toppled over it like a felled tree.

"Watch your step," Kate crooned sweetly through the canvas. With a strangled oath, Larry regained his feet and charged off in the direction of his house.

Kate and Aunt Melindy rocked with laughter. Each time they tried to speak they went off in new gales. Finally they managed to crawl out of the sagging tent and survey the damage. "Just three ropes," said Kate. "They'll be easy to fix." She waved at Rooney's house, in case Larry was looking. "He's been pretty good lately," she said. "Guess he had a relapse."

They gathered up their gear and went inside. Kate's mother was just coming down from her workroom. "Well are you two rested after your morning's excitement?" she asked with a smile at their disheveled appearance.

"My body is rested, my soul refreshed," announced Aunt Melindy. "This has been a day to celebrate.

I am going to go home and change into my own clothes, my very best ones. Then if you would all be so kind as to come by for me at seven, we will dine at Longwood Inn. My treat."

T HE NEXT MORNING Kate went on the train with her father to Newberry Junior College to help him prepare his classroom for the returning students. While they were pottering about, Mr. Krantz from the economics department wandered in and was soon sharing his latest tips on investing with Kate's father.

"Coins are the way to go, Jim," he said seriously.

"I grab all that come my way," replied Kate's father, equally serious.

"Really?" began Mr. Krantz eagerly, then, "Oh, you jest. I mean collectors' coins. That's a sure investment and the best place for your money these days."

"The problem of what to do with my money is usually solved for me at the grocery store," said Kate's father with a smile, "but I appreciate your tip. What do you do with these coins?"

"I just hang on to them. Keep them in a safe place, of course. You could use a safe deposit box, but I personally don't trust banks. Nor do I trust safes and other home storage methods. Between you and me, I bury them."

"Bury them?" Jim Sardis grinned. "Where do you store your treasure map?"

"I have my system," said Mr. Krantz mysteriously. "And I don't worry about theft, or fire, or . . ."

"What about earthquake?"

"We don't live in an earthquake area," replied Mr. Krantz a bit stiffly. He turned to leave. "If you ever want to get into it, I'll be glad to advise you."

"Awfully good of you," said Kate's father. "See you Monday."

"Where do you suppose he puts it?" Kate asked as soon as Mr. Krantz was gone.

"Probably in his back yard." Her father laughed. "Want to go over with shovels some night?"

Kate thought about the buried coins all the way home. She had always been interested in hidden or buried treasure. There was supposed to be lots of good stuff lying about on the bottoms of the oceans, just waiting to be found and make someone rich. Archaeologists were always digging up old treasures, too. But then, they knew where to look. She wondered why people weren't swarming all over Mr.

Krantz' yard whenever he wasn't around. If he had told Kate's father, he must surely have told others as well. Word of that sort tended to get around.

"People could tell where he'd dug," said Kate. She couldn't get her mind off the idea of all those coins scattered about just below the grass.

"I'm sure he has his system," her father answered vaguely from behind his newspaper. "Krantz doesn't have a little yard in town, you know. He lives on something more like an estate, out in the country."

Kate nodded. It figured. With all that buried wealth, he could afford an estate. Her father ought to listen to Mr. Krantz. Maybe they could get rich too.

After lunch Kate went up to her room. She was still thinking about burying things. For someone in her position, it had good points. *If* something did happen to her, she had a few things that she would like kept safe. Nothing valuable; those things would all go to family or friends. Alison would probably want her travel alarm clock and the birthstone ring Aunt Melindy had given her, Angie would like her embroidered backpack, Mike her marble collection, and everybody could divide up her books. But there were some other things important to her that would mean nothing to anyone else. Those would probably be thrown away unless she did something about it. Anyway, she'd often thought of burying a box of something. Now was the time.

Kate rummaged in the back of her closet until she found a round tin box that Christmas cookies had come in. It was a perfect box. The lid fit tightly, the metal would keep the moisture out, and there was a beautiful sleigh scene on the cover. Into the box she put a smile button, her ball-bearing shooter, a doll she'd made from cherry stems, her collection of baby teeth, a lock of her hair, her jackknife with the broken blade, a Canadian nickel and penny, and last year's cat calendar all folded up. She wrote: Kate Sardis, age 9, 148 Willow St., April 24 on a picture post card that she'd gotten at the ocean last summer and laid it on top. Then she pressed the lid down firmly and sealed it with masking tape.

It took a while to find the shovel. It was true no one ever put things back where they belonged. She finally found it behind the garage where she'd left it when she was digging worms for her fishing trip with Aunt Melindy.

Kate knew exactly where she was going to bury her box. There was a huge lilac bush in the corner by the dining room window where the house made an ell. Behind the bush and under the window was

Kate's secret hiding place. She could sit in there and look out, but nobody could see in.

It was hard digging back there because that was where the rain dripped off the roof and packed the earth down. Kate wanted the hole to be deep enough for security, but not so deep that she couldn't dig up the box every now and then to look at it, if she was around to do so.

Just when she was thinking that one or two more scoops would be enough, her shovel hit something hard. She thought it was a stone and wiggled the shovel to work around it, but whatever it was squeaked instead of scraped. She knelt and scooped the dirt out with her hands, until she uncovered a flat, dented surface. She worked her fingers around the edges, and after a lot of wiggling and tugging, finally pulled the thing free.

It was a box. A rectangular tin box, all brownish and rusty, although Kate could still see signs of printing on top. Things rattled when she shook it, but the lid was stuck. She practically ripped her fingernails off trying to open it, until she remembered the jackknife in her own box. It took a while to get at it through all the masking tape. She worked the broken blade around and around the edge of the lid, pried some more and finally got it loose.

Kate looked just long enough to see that the box held a collection of stuff like her own before she burst out through the lilac bush, around the house and into the kitchen.

"Mom, Dad!" she yelled. "Come quick! Look what I found!" Her mother rushed down from her workroom and her father banged in from the front porch. Kate put the box on the kitchen table. "It's a treasure box," she said, "and it was buried in the exact same place I was going to put mine."

"It's an old cigar box," her father said, examining the rusty metal. "My grandfather used to have some like it."

"Well what's in it?" Elizabeth Sardis asked her daughter. Excitement sparked in her eyes, and her mouth curved in anticipation. "Come on, Kate. Aren't you going to open it?"

"I already have," Kate answered. She took off the lid and began to remove the items, one at a time. There was a little harmonica on a string, a shell, two pennies, some marbles, a rusty Red Cross pin, a plastic dog glued to a magnet, and a moldy piece of paper, on which was printed:

Lila Higgins
148 Willow St.
Grade 5

August 14, 1949

Kate stared at the stuff. She couldn't believe it. A girl her age, who had probably lived in her house, had thought of a treasure box too and had put it in the same hiding place. It was like a dream, like something made up.

Her mother held the dog magnet in her hand. "I had two of these when I was a little girl," she said. "I used to make them chase each other across the table."

"What are you going to do with this, Kate?" her father asked.

"I'm going to put it back," said Kate. "But don't look where I go. It's our secret place."

They put the things into the box and pressed the lid down tight. Kate went back behind the lilac bush and sat for a long time with the two boxes in her lap. Then she got up and started digging again until the hole was wide enough to put the boxes in side-by-side. When the hole was filled in, she stamped the earth smooth and scattered twigs about, so that just Lila and she would know it had been dug.

"I ought to tell Krantz about this," her father said at supper. "Might give him second thoughts about the security of his system."

"Imagine," her mother said dreamily. "People

throughout the ages have left their treasures in the earth. It's an intriguing concept."

Kate just smiled. She was feeling hugely satisfied with her day's work. Aunt Melindy was right. It was good to get your affairs in order, no matter what.

O N FRIDAY MORNING, when Alison asked Kate to play chess, Kate found herself in the all-too-familiar situation of losing. No matter what game they played, Kate usually lost to Alison. Friday morning proved no different. As Kate was trapped in checkmate for the third straight game, her frustration sent the board flying and the pieces skipping across the floor.

"What's going on?" asked Kate's mother from the doorway.

"Oh, baby lost and threw the board on the floor," Alison said in disgust. "Some of the pieces went down the heat vent." She turned to Kate. "Fish them out, jerk. And make sure you find every one. You're not going to ruin this set like you did the last one."

"I didn't ruin the last set," shouted Kate. "And I'm not a baby."

"Oh yeah?" her sister answered. "You're a spoil-sport then. That's worse. Nobody likes a poor loser."

"Enough!" their mother said. "Pick up those pieces, Kate, and you go find something else to do, Alison. I don't know why you two play games together."

Kate felt close to tears with anger and frustration. She didn't want to be a poor sport. She didn't like them herself. When she beat Sammy Levin in a spelling contest at school, he had said that her words were easier and that Angie had whispered the last one to her. It wasn't true, but she didn't feel as happy about winning after he told that to everyone. And when she won Mike's shooter off him he had had such a fit she'd given it back and said she'd never play marbles with him again, which she wouldn't. So she didn't like poor sports either, but she couldn't help being one herself when she lost. No matter how hard she tried. Of course, she wouldn't act like that outside of her house, like Sammy and Mike did, because that was dumb. But she couldn't seem to control herself when she was playing with Alison.

Alison didn't help. She had this awful little smile whenever she won that made Kate want to shake her toothless. Losing wasn't so bad with kids her own age, like Angie and Mike, because sometimes they won and sometimes she did and that seemed fair. But Alison *always* won. And she smiled her horrible smile and then she got disgusted with Kate for being a poor sport.

"She's older than you are," said Kate's father. He was painting the railing next to the steps where Kate sat sunk in gloom. "What do you expect?"

"I expect to lose, since I always do," said Kate, "but I *hope* to win. If I didn't hope to win I wouldn't play."

"Winning isn't everything," her father said. "Playing is the important part. That's where the fun is."

"I'm interested in winning," said Kate. She wanted to remind her father that he hadn't seemed to be having much fun when her mother beat him at tennis, but decided it wasn't a good idea to bring that up.

"If winning is all you're interested in, then maybe you'd better not play Alison until you are older," her father said. "Then things will be more equal."

"I think I'm addicted," said Kate. "I keep telling myself not to play certain games with her and then I do it anyway. It's like a sickness."

"Maybe you can learn how to handle it," Kate's father suggested. "I don't think anybody really likes to lose, do you?"

"No," said Kate, "but I seem to have more trouble with it than most. Probably because I lose more than most. Then I have to worry about being a poor sport on top of it. Losing is bad enough without everyone noticing how you do it. And Alison always acts like I'm the only one with the problem."

"I don't imagine it's any easier for her," Jim Sardis said soothingly.

"She wouldn't know that," Kate responded sourly. "It's never happened to her."

Kate sat thinking on the steps a long time after her father had finished painting and gone off to other projects. This was something she wanted to settle once and for all. She remembered her mother reading from "Dear Abby" that there were no good losers, only good actors. Well, she would try to be a good actor then. But that wasn't enough. She wanted to beat Alison. Just once. Not at Old Maid or Sorry, or something that was mostly luck, but at a game that took skill. She wanted to prove to herself that she could do it, and she wanted Alison to see what it felt like to lose.

If Harlan Atwater, whom she was beginning to dislike very much, was right, she had better get at it. It could take a long time, and that was something she might not have. She decided to go for badminton. Alison liked that game, and it was something that Kate might have a chance in. Even though Alison was taller and had taken tennis lessons, Kate could be fast if she really concentrated. She couldn't spike them like Alison could, but maybe she could win on defense.

"Want to play badminton?" she asked her sister casually after lunch.

"Why would I want to play anything with you?" Alison replied coldly.

"Because you like the game. And you like to win. And I promise I won't say a word when I lose."

"Hah!" said her sister. Then, "Oh, all right. But if you throw a baby fit, I'll quit."

They got the set from the garage and put it up on the back lawn. It was the first time they had had it out that year and it took a while to untangle the net and ropes.

"We'll volley for serve," said Alison, and they were off. Alison took the first three games. Kate smiled gamely and won the fourth. Alison took two more, then Kate got another.

"You're really improving," Alison said. "Want to quit?" Kate's attitude was clearly puzzling her.

"Oh no," said Kate. "This is fun."

Alison won the next game, and then Kate won two. Alison stared grimly across the net as she served. For the first time her gaze acknowledged Kate as an equal competitor.

Kate, on her part, was concentrating. Every fiber

was focused on getting that birdie across the net, she didn't care how. She was so preoccupied with her task that she didn't respond one way or another to the score, other than to register businesslike satisfaction with her successes.

Suddenly, at the end of another win for Kate, Alison hurled her racket to the ground and stalked into the house. Kate stared after her in surprise. Then she retrieved her sister's racket and put it and the rest of the equipment away in the garage. She came out onto the driveway and looked down the street. The old red ice cream truck was creeping slowly in her direction. This was definitely the day to cash in her free stick. She'd get a grape Popsicle and split it with Alison. That might help her feel better.

Kate smiled as she dashed to get the stick. Things had changed. She knew that in a certain way they would never be quite the same again.

W HEN KATE BROUGHT the Popsicle to Alison, her sister did not turn from her desk.

"I brought you something," said Kate. She stood in the doorway, waiting for Alison to look up. When her sister acted like this, it was best to proceed cautiously.

After a few seconds, Alison glanced in her direction. "I'm not hungry," she said stiffly, and turned back to her desk.

"Well I got it for you with my free stick, so you have to eat it." Kate marched into the room and planted the popsicle in her sister's hand. Alison said nothing, but at least she didn't let it drop to the floor.

As they were washing for supper, Alison thanked Kate politely for the popsicle and then said no more to anyone all through dinner. Their parents didn't comment on her silence. They chatted with Kate about the garden, about Aunt Melindy leaving for New York to attend a rare book show, and about their own plans to spend that evening with friends.

When they left, Alison still hadn't said much, but she seemed more thoughtful than upset. The two girls watched television, read awhile, then went to bed early with their books.

"Good night, Alison," said Kate as they parted in the hall.

"Good night, Kate," Alison said in her normal voice, "and really, thanks for the Popsicle. It was my favorite kind."

Kate climbed into bed carefully, so as not to disturb Arthur who was already curled up at the bottom. She read until she felt sleepy, then reached to turn out her light. Without warning, her hand was suddenly clutching the sideboard of the bed frame instead of the light switch. The slat under the head of the bed had gotten out of position again and fallen to the floor, leaving the springs and mattress tilting crazily downward. Arthur rolled down the incline and landed on Kate's chest. He blinked with surprise, stood, stretched, then climbed up over the sideboard and headed with great dignity for his more reliable bed in the kitchen.

"Alison," called Kate with something between a wail and a giggle, "you've got to help me."

There was no answer. "Alison," Kate hollered, "I need you."

Alison came in, blinking in the light. "What's the matter?" she asked irritably. "You woke me up."

"What do you mean 'What's the matter?' Do you think I always sleep in this position?" Kate climbed out of the bed frame. "You have to help me lift the springs and mattress and get the slat back under them."

"Wait for Mom and Dad." Alison yawned and started back for her room.

"No no!" Kate stopped her. "Come on, Alison. We can do it. I want to go to bed, and Mom and Dad might not come home for hours."

"Oh all right," Alison said crossly, "but we'll do it my way. Do exactly what I tell you, okay?"

Kate nodded meekly. With a mighty effort, Alison grabbed hold of the top of the mattress and folded it back towards the foot of the bed.

"Now you hold this," she gasped, "and don't let go."

"Don't worry," Kate assured her. "I'll hold it." She leaned all her weight against the heavy mattress. It was harder to hold than she'd thought. The inner springs seemed to fight back. "Don't worry," she puffed more to herself than to her sister. "I won't let go."

"You'd better not," Alison said grimly, and bent over the bed to reach down through the springs for the fallen slat. Just as she was starting to lift it into position, Kate could feel the mattress slip. "Hurry up," she groaned, leaning her shoulder into the avalanching pad, but it was too late. The mattress sprang past her and settled with a resounding thud to its usual flat position on the bed.

Kate was horrified. Alison would kill her. Alison? There wasn't a sound from her. All Kate could see of her sister was her lower half sticking out from between the mattress and the collapsed springs.

Kate giggled. She shouldn't have. One giggle led to another until she was completely helpless with laughter. Tears poured down her face and still she howled. The sight of Alison's hind end protruding from the bed like sandwich stuffing was the funniest thing she'd ever seen.

"Get me out of here!" Even through the mattress, Alison's voice cut like steel.

"Don't worry. I'm trying," answered Kate, but her voice lacked conviction.

"Kate!" yelled Alison warningly, and with a huge

heave Kate managed to raise the mattress enough for Alison to back out.

"You did that on purpose!" Alison spluttered as soon as she was free. "I know you did that on purpose. Don't you ever ask me for help again, you little monster."

"I didn't," Kate protested. "I wouldn't do a thing like that on purpose." She was horrified to hear her voice break with more laughter.

Alison marched furiously from the room. "Hey Alison," Kate called after her. "I'm sorry. I couldn't help it. It was too heavy. Maybe if we put the mattress on the floor we could fix it."

"Put the mattress up the chimney if you like," came her sister's icy reply, "but don't say one more word to me." The house vibrated as Alison's door slammed shut.

Kate sighed as she dragged the mattress to the floor. Alison would probably wear a party hat to her funeral now. They might never speak again. She made up her mattress with pillow and blankets and crawled in. At least she had a clear conscience. She would never ask her sister for help and then deliberately knock her flat. Alison couldn't really believe that either. Kate giggled again, and then was asleep.

O NE DAY LEFT before I find out, Kate thought the minute she woke on Saturday morning. That idea sobered even her memories of why she was sleeping on the floor.

Her father came in. "I understand you and your sister had quite an evening," he said. "According to her you attacked her with a mattress." He grinned. "Come on. Let's get this thing back together."

When Kate went downstairs for breakfast, Alison had already left for her friend Carol's house. "Good," thought Kate grumpily. "Now I won't have to worry about offending royalty." She scowled at her oatmeal. She was tired of this day before it had even begun.

"You two girls must have eaten sullen snacks last night," her mother said as she poured Kate's milk.

"Come on now, you don't want to waste a beautiful day like this."

Kate sighed. Her mother was right. She must not waste today. But it was sure hard making the best of her time for so long.

She should do the things she really wanted to, Aunt Melindy had said. Well, she wasn't in the mood for it. She couldn't even think of anything she really wanted to do. Both Mike and Angie were gone until Sunday night, Aunt Melindy was away at the rare books show, and Alison would probably never play with her again.

Kate walked out into the bright sunshine. For a while she played Seven-Up against the garage wall, then she went to sit on the porch steps.

"Hope you trip on your brains," she muttered when Harlan Atwater went by on the opposite sidewalk. He walked like he had springs in his heels, bouncing up on his toes with each step. Why should she worry about what someone who walked like that said.

"I'm going for a little walk," Kate yelled to her parents through the screen door. She went up to the corner, over one block, then down River Street. She met no one she knew, which was just as well, because as soon as the grange came into sight Kate knew that that was where she had been heading.

The grange was an old white building about half-way down River Street. People used to go there for meetings, but now some of its windows were broken, and nobody cut the grass or went there anymore. Nobody, that is, except kids who played there and Sailor. Sailor went there to drink. He sat out back, leaning against the wall, and drank one bottle of whiskey after another. He stayed there all day sometimes, drinking and taking naps, then he would get up and go home. Kate didn't know where he lived. When she saw him, he was either sitting behind the grange or weaving down the sidewalk.

Mrs. Sardis didn't want Kate to play around the grange. There was lots of broken glass, and she knew about Sailor. He didn't like kids, because some of them, like Larry Rooney, teased him. Kate had peeked around the corner of the building once, just to see if he was there, and he had staggered up after her, yelling and waving his bottle. Kate had run home so fast she hadn't even looked when she crossed the street.

Sailor was never at the grange on Saturdays or Sundays, and that's when kids played there. What they did was jump off the roof. You could get to the roof by climbing a rusty fire escape that went up the side of the building to a second story door. If you stood on the railing of the fire escape, you could pull yourself onto the roof above the door. Then you crawled up to the peak, down the other side, and jumped off into the tall grass. Kate had watched kids do it, but she'd never done it herself. Partly because she wasn't supposed to play around the grange, but mostly because she was scared.

It was a big thing to jump off the grange roof. Kids respected you for it. Word got around when someone did it. "You know Timmy O'Brien? He jumped off the grange roof." Like that.

Kate had always wanted to achieve that fame. It was like a test she had set for herself. And now was the time.

She noticed with relief that no one was there. She didn't like to try new things with people watching. This way she could take her time.

Kate climbed the fire escape. She held on to the shaky rain spout and managed to get up on the railing. Carefully she transferred her grip from the spout to the roof edge. A wave of panic hit her as she teetered there, but it was too late to go back. With a huge effort she kicked and pulled herself up and over the roof edge. She rested for a little while, then crawled up the roof to the peak. It was much steeper than it looked from the ground.

Kate just lay on her stomach when she reached the peak. She was afraid she'd slide off if she sat up or moved around. The view was nice—she could see over to her own street—but she was too nervous to really enjoy it. She was also wondering how she was going to get down. Crawling up was hard enough, but crawling down toward a drop-off seemed impossible. She wondered if her parents would come looking for her if she hadn't managed by dark, and what they would say when they found her on the grange roof where she wasn't supposed to be.

After a lot of thinking, Kate decided the best thing to do would be to get down by herself. That way her parents wouldn't know, and she could tell Angie and Mike about it. They would be impressed. So would Alison. She had never done it.

It took Kate ages to back down the roof to the edge, which turned out to be the worst place yet. Kate figured she could either keep backing down on her stomach until she was dangling in space and then let go, or she could turn around, sit on the edge, and jump.

Neither choice seemed good, but Kate finally decided that she would rather see what she was heading for. Maybe one spot was better to aim for than another. On the count of three she could turn over, sit up, check out below, then wiggle down until her legs were over and jump.

Kate was actually up to sixty-seven before she

turned over and started to wiggle to the edge. One wiggle was all it took. She slid down and off before she knew what happened.

The tall grass was not as soft as it looked. It hid an old tire rim that caught Kate's elbow with a sickening snap as she landed. Kate's arm hurt so much she thought she was going to throw up. Dizziness swept her. She lay still until her head cleared, then cautiously moved her legs, which appeared undamaged except for scratches, and forced herself to stand. She had to get home, no matter how much it hurt. Clutching her injured arm to her chest to keep it from moving around, Kate headed for the sidewalk, tears of pain streaming down her face.

"Kate! Hey Kate, wait for me!" It was Alison, pedaling down River Street on her way home for lunch. At the sound of her sister's voice Kate's sobs increased, but she kept on going. She had to get home.

Alison was off her bike the minute she saw Kate's face. "What's the matter? What happened? Are you hurt?" she asked anxiously.

"My arm," was all Kate could sob. "I hurt my arm."

"I'll get Mom. Take it easy, Kate, I'll get Mom," and Alison was on her bike and off down the street, hunched over the handle bars in an effort to get there faster.

Kate kept walking, but in just a couple of minutes she saw her mother and Alison running up the sidewalk toward her. Her father was just behind in the car. The minute Mrs. Sardis saw Kate's arm, she knew it was broken. They drove to the hospital emergency room, with Alison wiping Kate's face and patting her knee the whole way.

No questions were asked until they were home again. Kate's arm was set and in a sling. It would be there, the doctor said, for six weeks. He had given her something to help the pain, but had warned that she would be uncomfortable for a few days.

"Tell me again what happened, Kate," Elizabeth Sardis said when she had tucked Kate into bed. The medicine and the whole experience had made Kate groggy.

"I jumped off the grange roof," Kate said. "My arm hit a tire rim."

"Why?"

"I wanted to prove I could do it," said Kate. "It seemed the right time."

Her mother nodded. She said no more, but she stayed by Kate's bed until she was asleep.

KATE WAS WAITED ON hand and foot for the rest of the day. Whenever she wasn't sleeping, her family hovered in attendance. Alison brought her an eclair from Larson's bakery, her father played gin with her, and television rules were relaxed.

But the next morning, even all the attention and her aching arm could not make Kate forget what day it was. It was Sunday, the day she had been waiting for all week. Today she would find out if there would be a tomorrow. Today she would know if Harlan Atwater was as smart as he seemed. Today she would be sure.

Or dead.

A great wave of terror swept Kate. She'd been thinking about this all week, but it hadn't been real. She hadn't really felt it. She hadn't really believed it. Even now the awful fear lessened as her mother brushed her long hair. Kate loved to have her hair brushed, after the tangles were out. She wasn't very careful about the tangles when she brushed it herself, so her mother had to work awhile this morning before the brush could sweep freely through Kate's bright brown hair.

The morning went swiftly and pleasantly enough. Alison fed Arthur for Kate, then they did crosswords. But as lunch approached, Kate became increasingly nervous. She looked at the clock so often that her mother asked if she was expecting someone.

"No," answered Kate. "Everyone's away."

"Do you have other plans?" her mother asked. "We were going to take you to the park, to get your mind off your arm, but if you have other plans . . ."

"I think I'd rather just stay here, thank you," said Kate. Somehow it seemed very important to be at home at 2:47 that afternoon.

Even though it might be her last meal, Kate couldn't eat much lunch. "Maybe you'll feel better at supper," her mother said. "We're picking Aunt Melindy up at the train at four-thirty and bringing her back here for chicken and dumplings."

The thought of the chicken and dumplings that might never get made, of Aunt Melindy getting off the train and being met with the sad news, of school starting tomorrow with her desk empty, was suddenly too much for Kate. As tears ran down her face, her mother asked in concern, "Does your arm hurt that much? The doctor gave us something you could take . . ."

Kate shook her head. "It's not that," she sobbed. "It's just . . ." Suddenly it came out. "I'm afraid of dying," she snuffled through her tears.

"Of dying? Kate honey, your arm may hurt, but it's not serious. It will get better."

"I know." Kate nodded miserably, and found she could say no more. It was just too confusing. Nothing could prove Harlan Atwater wrong, which would be her only comfort, but time itself. "Maybe I'm just tired," she said. "I think I'll go lie down in my room."

Alison came into the kitchen. "If you're going to rest, I guess I'll go over to Carol's for a little while," she said.

"Good-bye, Alison," Kate called in a quavery voice as her sister started out the door. "Thanks for everything."

Alison looked back in surprise. "Don't let it break you up," she said. "I'm just going around the corner."

If she only knew where I might be going, thought Kate sadly as she watched Alison pedal off down the driveway. She went up to her room and tried to read, but her eyes kept going to the clock. It was hard to think about anything else when you were facing death. She sat on her bed for a while, then in the living room, then on the porch steps. She would have had time for a visit with Aunt Melindy, if she had been home. That would have helped. Now she wouldn't even be able to say good-bye to her.

After what seemed forever, Kate went back into the house and looked at the clock. It was 2:30. Her insides felt squishy, and her lungs seemed to be disconnected. She went to her room and put all her stuffed animals together on her bed. She shut the closet door and put her roller skates side by side under the bureau. She closed her book on a bookmark, then went down to the kitchen to watch the hands of the electric clock. It was always more accurate than the one in her bedroom.

Kate sat at the table and arranged her upper body across it, with her head facing the clock. That at least should keep her from collapsing to the floor. She could hear her father raking outside and her mother humming upstairs in her workroom. She wanted to call out to them, to summon them, but time was going too swiftly now. Two minutes to go, one, then the second hand was sweeping up to the twelve again. Kate shut her eyes and gripped the edge of the table.

She opened one eye just as the second hand crossed the twelve. It went right on past and Kate was still there watching it.

She was not dead.

With a great surge of relief that brought tears to her eyes, Kate watched the hand go around several more times to be absolutely certain. Then she stood up and stretched as though she'd just gotten up from a long nap. She felt terrific. She couldn't stop smiling. Everything looked beautiful, the old wooden table with its pot of daffodils, the curtains fluttering in the spring breeze, Arthur's bed by the cellar door. Arthur. There he was, napping in the sun on the doormat. She was going to be there after all to love and feed him.

It was a funny thing. Kate had always hated asparagus, but when her mother cooked it for supper that night, nothing ever smelled so good, and it was Kate's favorite vegetable ever after.

K ATE DIDN'T TELL anyone about that week for quite a while. For one thing, it seemed pretty silly that she had ever believed Harlan Atwater. He might be smart, but nobody knew everything. When she told Alison about it, instead of laughing as she had expected, her sister got really mad at Harlan. She said he was weird and probably got his kicks scaring little kids. Not that Kate was that little anymore. She'd grown up a lot since that week of April vacation. Maybe because of it.

Her parents said she should have told them, that of course they didn't know everything, but things aren't usually so scary if you share them. Aunt Melindy said she didn't see much difference between what happened to Kate and what happened to a lot of grown-ups she knew who spent their lives fearing that every twinge was a heart attack and every wheeze terminal pneumonia. "Death can get you any time," she said. "You can be proud that you didn't just sit around waiting for it."

The credit for that, Kate knew, went to Aunt Melindy and her advice. Because of it, that week had changed Kate's life. In good ways. She now had a cat, and her mother hadn't gotten one single flea bite since Arthur came. She had found an unusual friend of another generation with whom she shared a secret of treasure boxes. She had beaten Alison and gotten better at losing, and she had jumped, after a fashion, off the grange roof. The results of that, to be sure, had been rather painful, but the kids at school were gratifyingly impressed. There was something dashing about an arm in a sling, provided you hadn't broken it in some dumb way like falling out of bed.

And last but not least, the idea of death, as long as it was not actually staring her in the face, was no longer as fearful to Kate as it had been. After all, Aunt Melindy was eighty-two. If she didn't worry, why should Kate?

ABOUT THE AUTHOR

Ruth Wallace-Brodeur grew up in western Massachusetts and received her B.A. from the University of Massachusetts. Childhood summer vacations, which were spent camping on a pasture hill in northern Vermont, combined with tales of her father's Canadian youth to provide background for *The Kenton Year,* her first book, followed now by her second, *One April Vacation*. Ruth Wallace-Brodeur lives in Montpelier, Vermont, with her husband, Paul, and their four children, Jennifer, Jeremy, Rachel and Sarah.